I WAS RETURNING FROM PUB, FRIDAY NIGHT. SO MUCH TO ENJOY. IT WAS LATE. FOUND A STRANGER GIRL CROSSING ROAD RUTHLESSLY, AND HAD ACCIDENT, AND SHE WAS SENSELESS. BOUGHT HER TO MY APARTMENT. WAKING UP SHE WAS ALL BLURRY, CAN'T REMEMBER ANYTHING. AFTER SOME FOOD AND REST SHE STARTED TO REMEMBER HER LIFE AND START TALKING...

AARGH!
HELLO!
IT SEEMS SHE WAS DIZZY AFTER A LONG NAP!!
WHO ARE YOU? DO I KNOW YOU?

all seems blurry

Where Am I?
I don't remember.....
I found her last night when returning from pub after a friday night.....

you were lucky...car hitted you. but you were safe don't know how... the driver helped me carrying you in my apartment...you were senseless...
Thought to call the police... but if you r from this city... you know how that would work...

last night I was returning from pub. you know?.. friday night... so much to enjoy...it was late

night was deep and cars are ruthless. you might be drunk or mad I don't know....You were running towards a speedy car..

police would probably hold me for night. and I didn't found any docs in your bags and pockets...not even your mobile...so you can guess... they would probably hold you too...for d night...

Don't worry, I didn't do anything to you while you were asleep
tell me your story now!!

my head still hurting...I can't...

It's ok.. take some rest.. u hungry???

I think I'm... Thank you by d way..

It's nothing..anyone would do the same.. don't you think??

I don't know... It's all blank in my head..sorry!!

why you helping me?
this is strange in this city..
specially to strangers..!

you seems to be a nice
guy...I'm feeling a bit
better now....

It was still raining outside
like last night...a perfect weather
to stay at home!!

I was making food for her..
and for me also..she was still
in shock..I guess...

She was desparately tryinh
to recall things...I can tell by
her posture....!!

Did you remember anything?
Let's have food and talk...

we started to eat..

she seemed settled down
a bit...she was really
hungry...!!

I am Jenny..by d way..
It's all coming to me now..
I think I know what happened..

She started to crying after food...
It's better Not to drag you in my life.. I'll be leaving now...

You're not going anywhere.. I am happy to listen to you.. after all you r stranger here..
I am all alone...today's saturday.. no job...so ..I have time.. of course it's ur decision.. not forcing you...

she waited and stair to me for some time...gave a lucid smile...and started...

we had a happy family...in village. husband a farmer with horses..gardening.. farming..had our little angel..a daughter.
Monica she is...she was always happy... no demand...nothing..we r really happy..

we were always happy...

She was so jolly..
and playful..our little angel..

she learnt to ride cycle almost on her own.. so much energy..

she laughed so much and cried less from baby age..

learnt to make food with me..at that little age..

learnt draw beautifully every time...

school teacher's favourite was my daughter...she was so much more....

one day it's all changed...
all gone...

my husband was murdered
in a bar fight...he was not much
of a drinker...but that day ...
he gone to enjoy our kid's
top score in school...

it changes everything in our life,
he was murdered by just a
petty cause...and no one there
helped him...not even after death...

Police were there...but couldn't find the murderer
till now...maybe they didn't want to...bcoz
murderer was a local mafia...and my husband was
only a low life farmer...

loosing her father...my kid gone to depression
too...I couldn't help her...kid in her age are
so sensitive...her all happiness was gone...

when friends started bullying
her by saying..."fighter's kid"...coz her father
couldn't fight and win...it was enough for her...
she hanged herself when I was gone for bath...

All end..
No kid..no husband..
no family..no job..
nothing...relatives helps
was so pathetic....

sold the farm and house..
left that horrible place..
came to city..to have some
earning on my own..

2 years gone now..
I couldn't live this way..
the incidents still haunts
me..!!

I was too careless of my life..I think.. when you met me last night...I am really sorry.. and also thank you so much..

Let's sleep for today... let ur mimd rest. You'r safe now..

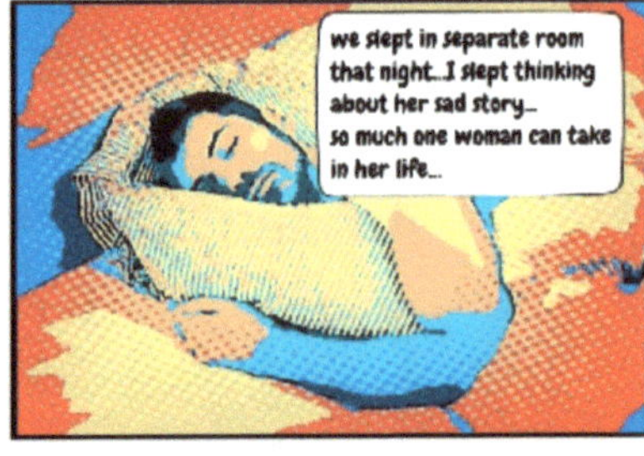

we slept in separate room that night...I slept thinking about her sad story... so much one woman can take in her life...

she also slept in deep.. at least I thought that way

but, I was wrong
completely... in deep
night she tried to kill me
by a flower vase..when
I was sleeping...

luckily I was strong
enough to awake before
it's done..and resisted in
shock!!

it seems..she was a thief
and murderer or fraud..
don't know exactly what!!!

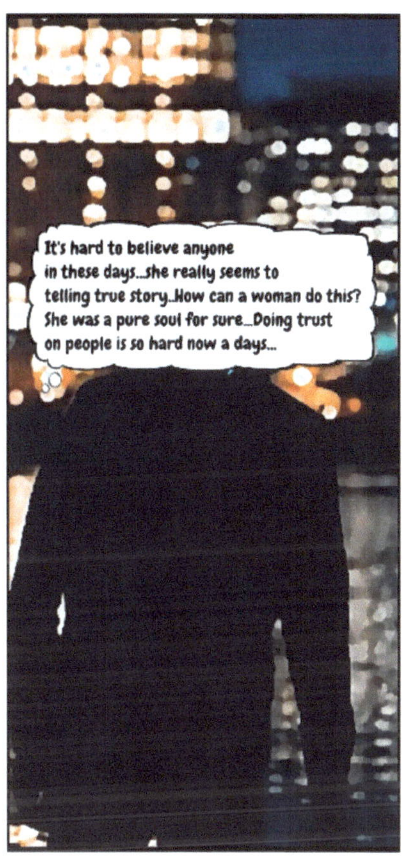
It's hard to believe anyone in these days...she really seems to telling true story..How can a woman do this? She was a pure soul for sure...Doing trust on people is so hard now a days...

but this story is different.... and I was in control of this story

I was a police guard for 5 years..and gave some exams..did some more learning.. become a police junior detective...

2 years of hard work more I become chief detective of department....

Not much age though.. sometimes other's r jealous that what I achieve in this young age..

Some years back.. there was a serial killer. killing Police officers.. one by one..no motive.. no connection...nothing

forensic told us that.. it was a lady everytime. no match to database.. anywhere...she was killing police officers..and robbing them

the case was getting lost day by day...who will be next victim..no one know.. but...we didn't know how she was getting info about police and whatnot....!!

until one day...
I found this lady's husband
closed case...I told myself...
this can be the cause...

I found out about
her life history, her records,
her current life, her depression...
and all...

I agree...she lost her all,
and her husband's case
closing was not justice...
not at all!!

but it was enough,
I needed to stop her
revenge...on whole
police department..

I was following her for long time...she was not making her move...

so, that night I make my move with her...that night I act like I found her...
accident was my making...It was my partner in department... the driver....

we talked as police, let her hear that we are police... I knew she was gonna act as faint and try to do her thing as other murders she did...

and it worked as planned
she did what she had to do in her conscience...

She theft...she robbed... then tried to kill me as planned...she didn't know I was awake....!! she failed and flew...

I had all planned...
I searched inside her purse,
and remove one knife when she was
inside bathroom.
removed all my knives from kitchen
as well before gone to bed...

she had no idea right now
in her den, I mean her apartment
my partner is waiting there..
until I reach...

We were right...Finally
she get caught..with the
theft and robbed things
from my apartment....

I reached and took a
confession out of her...

My partner and I
only know about her
this far...did a full
secrecy with whole
department...!!

she cried out and begged
for mercy...

I was not sure what to do now...as well as my partner...story was not end here...One thing I haven't told you yet...

Right or wrong both were in competition... I sent my partner to home, I can trust him fully...this decisions are from both of us...

I'm sorry for what happened to you and your family...I am really sorry...

I'm sorry from my whole department... Now when I know all... I'll try very much to reopen your case in time...

but, you need to leave this place...and this country too...you have murdered many police officers you know...

I'm sorry too... It's all hurts too much

I know you daughter is alive!!... I know in time of suicide she hurt herself badly.. and for her medical bill.. you need all the money...

I checked your bank, you didn't spent even single theft penny for yourself...

she is all I have...

I can understand,
any mother would
do that... you really
are a great mother..

I have managed to make
two of yours passport
and visa...you have to go from here..
It won't bring back
your husband...
If you go to jail...
what will be of your
daughter??

I know it's hard...but this
is the only way..I will say to
department that I lost you.
PASSEPORT

pack your belonging... and
please..let go of this revenge..
I am really sorry again..

I know I did wrong by letting go of this killer...but don't know...It felt right!! Damn right.

2 days later...
Gone to give her the last msg

left her a note and flowers.. may be her humanity still there..

wished her mother's day.. and told her that.."I really liked her in that night".. deep down everyone wants love may be...!!
Happy Mother's Day
SEE YA!

Needed to give her the
feeling, that not every
person is bad in this world..

and as per our talk, she really left this place after 4 days...

I don't know why I actually did it...
The End